Written by
Joy Pumar

To the journey of a young Aries full of fire,
may you find joy in everything you do.

– Joy Pumar

Published in association with
Bear With Us Productions

ISBN: 979-8-218-07174-5

Design by Luisa Moschetti
Illustrated by Laura Natali

www.justbearwithus.com

Illustrated by
Laura Natali

Hey, Young Aries!

How to be you!

Written by
Joy Pumar

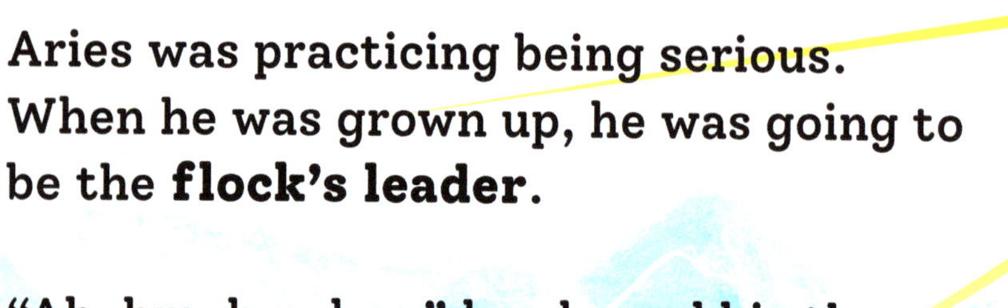

Aries was practicing being serious. When he was grown up, he was going to be the **flock's leader**.

"Ah-hm-hm-hm," he cleared his throat, imagining everyone looking at him.

"I'm Aries, your leader!" He made his voice as deep as he could. **"And I'll keep you safe."**

He couldn't help it—his voice squeaked on the word "safe". Being leader was a great honor, but Aries was a little bit scared.

He began to pace on his imaginary stage. "I will keep you safe from—um—**bees**..."

Aries had been stung when he was a tiny lamb and he hadn't liked that at all. As he walked on his stage, thinking about bees, he tripped and fell.

Oof! He rolled over and over, right down to the bottom of the little hill.

CLUNK! Something hard stopped his roll. Aries opened his eyes and saw... "Hey, Young Aries," said the large, menacing figure in front of him.

"Old Aries!" he gasped, scrambling to his feet and backing away nervously. Old Aries was the current leader.

"What are you up to, Young Aries?" asked Old Aries, smiling at him. "I was watching you from over there."

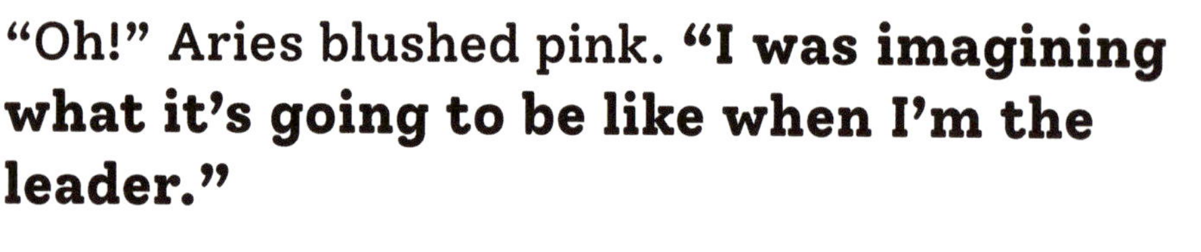

"Oh!" Aries blushed pink. **"I was imagining what it's going to be like when I'm the leader."**

"I see," said Old Aries thoughtfully. "I remember when I was your age, and I found out that I was to be leader."

He paused for quite a long time, then added, “I was very worried about it all, to be honest.”

“Really?” Aries was astonished.

“Oh yes!” exclaimed Old Aries with a smile. “I wasn’t as big and clever as I am now, and I worried that no one would listen to me.”

That was exactly how Aries was feeling! "What... what did you do about it?" he asked.

"Grandpa Aries, who was the leader then, took me to find **my animal guides**. There were six of them. I think the time has come for me to teach you the same thing—what do you think?"

"Yes, please!" Aries happily squeaked.

They set off, climbing a nearby mountain. As they went, Old Aries explained about animal guides.

"Every character trait is associated with an animal," he began.

"And if you find animal guides that are associated with the traits that you most wish you had, then, in time, you will find it easier to be the leader that you hope to be."

"Cool," said Aries. "So if I want to be really brave...?"

"Hmm," Old Aries thought aloud as he jumped from rock to crag. "You must find a **spirit tiger** for fearlessness."

“A tiger—oh!” Aries nearly tripped over again in surprise. “Aren’t tigers big and scary?”

Old Aries laughed, but quite kindly. “Yes, they can be. Shall we start small and work our way up to tigers?”

"Yes, please."

"Let's see now. That beautiful flowering shrub over there is the place. Go find your first guide."

"How will I know?"

"You will know."
Old Aries' voice was calm, and it gave Aries confidence to step over to the flowering plant that grew taller than his head.

He stood there for a moment, looking around.

WHOOSH!

A tiny emerald green something whizzed past him. A few leaves shook slightly.

WHOOSH! WHOOSH!

Two more somethings—these ones bright red and fiery orange, zoomed into the shrub.

“Whoa!” exclaimed Aries. “Who’s there?”

He peered between the branches and flowers and saw three tiny birds, no bigger than a lamb's hoof. They were flitting quickly from flower to flower, their wings beating so fast it sounded like a hum.

"Hummingbirds!" he breathed. "Hello!" A buzz from behind him made him turn.

A bright blue hummingbird was hovering there, looking at him. Suddenly, Aries felt excited and playful, as though he was having the best fun. He was filled with energy too, and wanted to run and jump all over the mountain.

“Is that you?” he asked.
“Are you my animal guide?”

The blue hummingbird buzzed, then flew away so fast that a shadowy outline of itself was left behind. Aries somehow knew what to do, and pushed his head into the outline.

It felt as though cool water had splashed over his face. He knew he had found his first animal guide.

He returned to Old Aries with a big smile on his little face.

"I can see you were successful," mused Old Aries. "Let us continue."

Next, Aries had to stand on the very edge of a cliff while hawks circled around him. One of them flew down towards him and made eye contact.

Aries felt as though he had been filled up with **power, strength, and confidence,** just like a coffee pot being filled with coffee. He almost felt brave enough to carry on by himself.

Old Aries chuckled when Aries told him that. “I remember my hawk too. I was sure I could do anything. Just as when Grandpa Aries was with me—I nearly fell down a crevasse!”

"What's next?" asked Aries. He liked feeling strong and confident, and playful and happy.

"Your **cheetah**, I think," said Old Aries. He walked a few paces before he realized that Aries had stopped. "What is it?"

"I don't like cheating," said Aries.

Old Aries laughed so much that he could hardly explain what a cheetah was.

By the time he had finished explaining, they arrived, and a beautiful cheetah with a long fluffy tail was walking up to Aries.

Her shadowy outline was warming, **and he felt like a leader for the first time.**

He was also superfast and raced Old Aries up the next section of the mountain. An eerie howl rose all around them as a cold mist closed in.

"W- wolves?" asked Aries.

"Yes," said Old Aries. "Draw on your new animal guides: you will need them to face up to a **wolf**."

Aries closed his eyes and concentrated on the hawk–fierce, independent, strong. And the cheetah–fast and authoritative.

Then, as he opened his eyes to find himself nose to nose with a real live wolf, his playful hummingbird trait popped up and he licked the wolf's nose!

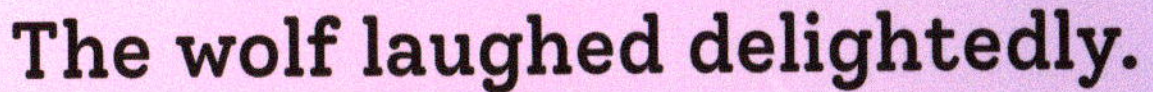
The wolf laughed delightedly.

"Oh, well done, little lamb!" he said. "It will be an honor to be your animal guide." The wolf's outline was furry and strong, and **Aries felt a pull towards his family and all the sheep in the flock.**

"That's because wolves are very loyal," said Old Aries. "They love their families more than anything."

Next up was a tiger.

"I feel braver and stronger than I did at the beginning," said Aries. "But I'm not sure if I'm ready for a tiger yet..."

"Of course, you are!" Old Aries replied. "Remember, your animal guides are with you all the time now."

When they found the tiger, he was snoozing under a tree, lazily licking one front paw.

“Hello,” managed Aries.

“Hi,” said the tiger, breathing out an outline for him to step into. Aries immediately felt as though **he was ready for anything**.

“Wow, tiger power!” he exclaimed.

"But, Old Aries?"

"Yes, youngster?"

"Didn't you say there were six animal guides?"

"I did." Old Aries smiled. "And the last one is a ram."

"Oh!" said Aries. "Who?"

"Me," Old Aries said coolly. Then he suddenly jumped to the side, leaving an outline for Aries to step into.

He did so. “There,” said Old Aries.

“Now you are prepared for whatever life throws at you. With your strength and your animal guides, you can do anything at all.” And that was quite true!

www.ingramcontent.com/pod-product-compliance
Ingram Content Group UK Ltd.
Pitfield, Milton Keynes, MK11 3LW, UK
UKHW060114300726
14090UKWH00002B/192
9781088185117